# fergus and the Night-demon

## an irish ghost story

by jim murphy

illustrated by john manders

Clarion Books / New York

Once, many years before you or I were even born, there lived in Ireland a lad named Fergus O'Mara. Now, Fergus was very good at a great many things, but working hard was not one of them.

"Fetch some peat for the fire," his dear mother said as she bent over the washtub.

"Ah, but Mother," Fergus answered, as he gobbled down the last morsel of his kidney-and-turnip stew, "the peat is so dirty, and I've my visiting clothes on tonight."

"Then bring in the cow and milk her," his mother said.

"The pasture is terrible muddy, and me in my best boots," Fergus replied as he opened the door.

"You are a lazy, good-for-nothing lad," his mother scolded. "One day you'll answer for your ways."

"Perhaps, Mother," said Fergus, "but tonight I'm off to Skibbereen for a bit of play."

Fergus chuckled as he walked up the narrow path. *Why worry about peat or the cow,* he told himself, *when I've coins in my pocket and plenty of time to spend them?*

Over a hill he went, then down along its steep shoulder, one long stride after the other. His belly bulged and ached from his hastily eaten supper, but that did not slow Fergus one bit. Not with a good time only a few miles away.

Then he came round a bend in the path and stopped dead in his tracks. There before him stood a great, tall creature.

"It is your time, Fergus O'Mara!" the creature hissed. It pointed
a bony finger at him.

The creature's tattered cloak fluttered in the breeze, and in its
left hand it held a long scythe. Two fiery eyes stared from under a
dark hood like glowing embers of peat. So horrible was the creature
that the lad's aching belly did a painful flip-flop.

Fergus trembled a moment or two in his fine boots. Then he realized something.

"Why, you are nothing but a silly dream caused by that garlic sausage I ate at breakfast." He ducked under the creature's outstretched arm. "Now, be gone with you."

On Fergus hurried across rolling fields of barley. A cold, angry
wind swept along the path, and Fergus had to pull his cap lower to
keep the dust from his eyes.

When he looked up, the creature stood before him again. This time it was twice as big as before.

"*It is your time, Fergus O'Mara!*" the creature said loudly. It held its scythe out so that Fergus could see the sharp, gleaming blade.

"If you are not that garlic sausage," Fergus cried, "then you must be the onion pie I had at noon! Yes, that's all that you are!"

The creature's eyes glowered and glowed. Then in a blink it swung the scythe at Fergus. But Fergus leaped up and over the hissing steel.

When he landed, he danced around the creature and
continued his journey.

The night sky rumbled and thundered and rumbled some more. Lightning flashed and made sharp and strange shadows on the twisting path. Suddenly, the gigantic creature loomed up in front of the lad.

"IT IS YOUR TIME, FERGUS O'MARA!" it said in a voice that shook the very earth Fergus stood upon.

Fergus looked right up into the burning eyes of the creature. "If you aren't the garlic sausage or the onion pie," Fergus said, "then surely you must be that stew I had for supper!"

There was another crack of lightning, which seemed to come from the creature's fierce eyes. Then a foot as big as the cottage Fergus and his mother lived in rose up and went to step on the tiny Fergus.

Down that foot came so hard, the stones in the ground popped up and went rolling here and there like so many marbles. But Fergus was a quick lad, and he jumped to the side to avoid being crushed, then scurried between the giant creature's legs.

"Now, stop that!" Fergus yelled over his shoulder. "I must get to Skibbereen and don't want any more of your tricks."

A cold rain started to fall just as Fergus saw the lights of the town ahead. That was when a dark shape began unfolding itself before the lad's astonished eyes. Up and up it rose, growing bigger and bigger, till it was taller than any mountain Fergus had ever seen. So big was the creature that it blocked the path to Skibbereen.

When Fergus saw that he could not get to town and his play, he grew very angry. Right up to the gigantic creature he ran. "Now, listen to me, you big pudding-headed—"

16

Before he could finish his words, the creature raised its scythe to touch the very clouds. Bolts of lightning flashed from every part of the scythe. The wind shrieked and wailed, and rain fell so hard that the path turned into a rushing stream.

Fergus took a step back, for he realized now that it was not his over-stuffed stomach that was haunting him. It was the terrible Night-Demon itself come for him.

"What . . . what is it you want from the likes of me?" asked the lad.

The Night-Demon said not a word but pointed to a place by the side of the path. Fergus's eyes grew wide with alarm when he saw that the demon was pointing to a tiny graveyard. The words on one headstone stood out in a flash of lightning: HERE LIES FERGUS O'MARA, A LAZY, GOOD-FOR-NOTHING LAD.

"Dig, Fergus O'Mara!" the Night-Demon commanded.

Fergus couldn't run round the Night-Demon to the safety of the town, and there was no place to hide in the wide-open countryside. So he entered the graveyard, and with shaking hands he took up the shovel leaning against the headstone.

Fergus pushed the shovel into the ground and lifted out a heaping scoop of dirt. Oh, and was that shovel heavy! He dug out a second shovel of dirt. This one was even heavier than the first.

*Now, this is not right,* Fergus thought. *Much more of this digging and my arms will fall off. But what can I possibly do to be rid of this hard work?* As he put the shovel in once again, a tiny idea came to him.

"With all due respect, sir," Fergus said to the Night-Demon, "you are making a terrible mistake here. For I am not the lazy Fergus O'Mara this grave is meant for."

The Night-Demon stirred the clouds with its scythe till the noise of the storm nearly drowned out the lad's words.

"You don't believe me?" Fergus asked. "Well, think on this.
Would a lazy, good-for-nothing lad walk from his cozy home
all the way to Skibbereen on a cold and stormy night?"

The Night-Demon stopped stirring the sky to listen.

"'No' is the answer you're looking for," Fergus said. "And would a lazy lad dance left and right and leap over a swinging blade to get past you? The answer is 'No' again."

The Night-Demon lowered its scythe, and the storm began to ease.

"And would a lazy lad dig his own grave so very carefully?" Fergus stepped out of the grave and shook his head. "Of course not. So you see, I am not the Fergus O'Mara that this grave belongs to, oh, no, I am not."

The Night-Demon's eyes were not glowing so fiercely anymore.

Fergus pointed across the graveyard toward a distant mountain. "The lazy Fergus O'Mara you seek lives beyond the Glandore Mountains in Clonakilty, some twenty miles off."

For the first time, the Night-Demon took its eyes off Fergus and looked in the direction of Clonakilty. Then it howled angrily and began to swirl round and round, pulling up sticks and leaves and Fergus's cap and even the shovel in his hands. Then off the great whirling storm roared to seek out the true owner of the grave.

Fergus wasted not a moment. Out of the graveyard he ran, and he did not stop till he was home. Quick as lightning, he brought in the cow and had her milked, then he gathered up a supply of peat and had a warm fire burning in the hearth.

"Why, Fergus," his surprised mother said when she saw her son rushing from one task to the other, "whatever has possessed you this night?"

"Nothing at all, Mother, nothing at all!" he replied. "But I promise to be the hardest working lad hereabouts, or my name is not Fergus O'Mara."

And he was indeed hard working from that night forward. For he knew that when the Night-Demon did not find a lazy Fergus O'Mara in Clonakilty, it would return to seek one along the path to Skibbereen.

# a note about this story

Ireland is a land populated by all sorts of magical creatures—ghosts and goblins, giants and little people. Most of these phantoms are fairly harmless, and many will actually do you a good turn if you are kind to them. Give food to the *Fear-Gorta,* the Hungry-Man, during times of famine, and he will bring you good luck. But others can be very nasty, especially to people who are cruel, untrustworthy, or lazy.

Fergus O'Mara is a very lazy boy indeed, more intent on what the Irish refer to as his *kailee,* his night visit, than on helping his weary mother around the farm. Traditionally, a character like Fergus would meet a spirit, or spirits, and in some way or other be frightened into repenting his sins. For this chore, I created the Night-Demon. The Night-Demon is a combination of the dreaded *Dullahan,* a headless phantom who takes his victims off in a black coach, and a particularly mean collection of goblins known as air-demons, who inhabit the clouds and mists.

It didn't seem fair to pit a mere human against any creature with magical powers. So I decided to make Fergus so determined to get to his play and so very hardheaded that he can completely ignore the terror before him. Naturally, each time he dismisses the Night-Demon, its anger and frustration—and its body—grow bigger and bigger, until it is too huge for even Fergus to ignore.

At this point, it looked as if the lad's fate was truly sealed and the story was over. Which set me to thinking: Will his punishment be too severe for his crime? If so, what should I do? That was when I thought to give Fergus a real gift, one to match that of any wily *leprechaun*—the ability to think and talk fast.

At first he uses this gift to get out of work, and then to convince himself that the Night-Demon is only a figment of his imagination and overstuffed stomach. Eventually, he uses it to confuse and escape the terrible Night-Demon.

This ending seemed just. Fergus has outwitted a more powerful enemy and escaped without a scratch, but he has also mended his lazy, good-for-nothing ways. Of course, Fergus is human, and as such he will probably be tempted to ignore his chores for another *kailee* sometime in the future. And when that happens, will he be confronted again by the Night-Demon or some other wandering spirit? And will his clever ways work a second time? To be honest, I don't know. But I'm sure that if you think long enough on it, you will. Just close your eyes and imagine a dark night, a winding road, and a lone traveler. . . .

———————

**To Carol and Tom Walsh—in remembrance of *kailees* past, and in anticipation of more in the future
—Jim Murphy**

**For Emilio and Nick, two likely lads
—John Manders**

Clarion Books
a Houghton Mifflin Company imprint
215 Park Avenue South, New York, NY 10003
Text copyright © 2006 by Jim Murphy
Illustrations copyright © 2006 by John Manders
The illustrations were executed in gouache and colored pencil.
The text was set in 16.5-point Loire.
www.clarionbooks.com
Printed in Singapore

*Library of Congress Cataloging-in-Publication Data*
Murphy, Jim, 1947– Fergus and the Night-Demon : an Irish ghost story / by Jim Murphy ; illustrated by John Manders.
p. cm. Summary: On his way to town to have some fun, a lazy but clever young man faces a terrible demon, who declares that his time has come.
ISBN-13: 978-0-618-33955-6   ISBN-10: 0-618-33955-8
[1. Laziness—Fiction.  2. Conduct of life—Fiction.
3. Demonology—Fiction. 4. Ireland—Fiction.]
I. Manders, John, ill.  II. Title.
PZ7.M9535Fer 2006   [Fic]—dc22
2005036539

TWP  10  9  8  7  6  5  4  3  2  1